Skiing:

THE REAL SKIER'S DICTIONARY
BY MORTEN LUND

ILLUSTRATIONS BY BOB CRAM

CORNERSTONE LIBRARY
Published by Simon & Schuster, Inc.
New York

Published by Cornerstone Library
A Division of Simon & Schuster, Inc.
Simon & Schuster Building
Rockefeller Center
1230 Avenue of the Americas
New York, New York 10020

CORNERSTONE LIBRARY and colophon are registered
trademarks of Simon & Schuster, Inc.

10 9 8 7 6 5 4 3 2

Manufactured in the United States of America

ISBN: 0-346-12630-4

Dedication:

*For neophytes, nymphets, tyros, turkeys, tourists, flakes,
hot dogs, intermediaries, advancing, expert racers,
rakehells, heliskiers, powderpigs, prigs
—for all those keen people who ski
and would like to be able to
laugh at
it.*

A Word About This Dictionary

Use this book well: many such dictionaries, after having been bought or given as presents, fall behind the sofa with old half-used bars of wax or get tucked under large volumes of bound *Playboy* magazines. You as a skier would be the worse for it, and probably break a leg, if you did something as stupid as mislay this book, rather than showing it to your friends who might want to buy a copy.

If someone has given you this book, *don't* say, "Why do I need a *ski dictionary*, for God's sake!" The truth is, you simply don't know, do you? Not only can this book make you well-spoken on the subject of the sport, but it can serve as a handy excuse to go back to the lodge or condo when you happen to develop a terrible hangover and can't shake it. Simply tell everyone that you feel irresistibly drawn to finish the letter "R" this weekend, and excuse yourself politely from "the crowd," who will be envious of someone owning such a treasury of information. Will anyone else besides you, the owner of this book, be able to squint knowingly across the slope and say, "Now if he'd only soften up his reploiement, just a bit!?"

This book might eventually make it possible for you to develop a marvelous reputation as a skier without actually going on the slopes at all.

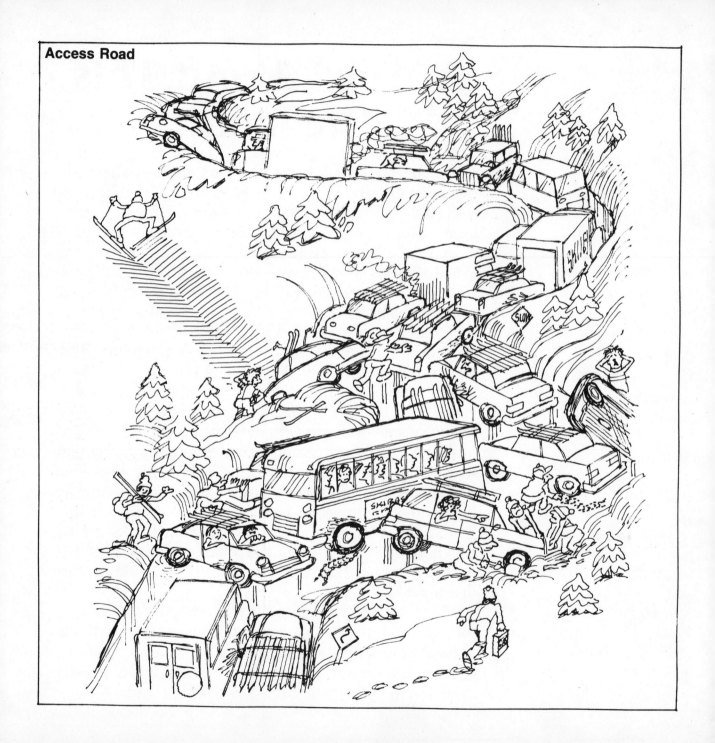

A

a real skier

any person who takes unfailing advantage of the sport's exceptional opportunities to smoke, drink, carouse, and ventilate the heat of sexual arousal. A real skier runs his body down to a degree impossible when simply staying home to watch reruns of *Dallas*.

access road

route leading to a resort from a public highway, engineered to minimize traffic, ensuring uncrowded skiing for resort personnel. Its design is limited only by the imagination of the builders and may incorporate gaping potholes, icy corners, tortuous switchbacks, downed electrical wires, partial blockage by snowdrifts, frost heaves, forty-five degree uphills and short, steep descents followed by sharp curves falling toward an outside shoulder that lacks any hint of guardrails.

alcohol

active ingredient of wine, beer, and hard liquor. It enables a skier to live through "slumps" during which the technique of turning becomes subtly elusive. Often called "the lubricant of skiing."

alpine combined

latest technical frill that starts with a prolonged bout of lovemaking immediately followed by an alpine race. This combination creates a euphoria that speeds the racer halfway down the course before he can choke up.

altitude

skier's state of mind: *high altitude* occurs when a skier, rightly or wrongly, imagines he is finally gaining expertise in skiing; *altitude sickness* occurs when a skier botches the first two turns on the first run of a big weekend.

ambience	verb frequently used by Southern snowbunnies when calling home from resorts, "Ambience so good. Ah really am."
Americans	people noted for heedless behavior on the slopes in Europe, as well as a thoroughgoing inability to comprehend simple foreign words; younger ones frequently offer "smokes" in exchange for lift passes; older ones normally offer candy bars or silk stockings.
an "A" class	group of "never-nevers," first-time skiers; they can eventually become members of more advanced "B" and "C" classes—without, however, much hope of ever getting into "D," "E," or "F" classes for really good skiers. The overall lesson structure everywhere in the world is made, quite deliberately, confusing—so as to preserve the superiority of a small elite; without this, much of the sport's appeal would be lost. So, do not be overly concerned if, in an "A" class, you find yourself following instructions you instinctively know are harmful, being given by an instructor whose judgment you have reason to suspect is whacko. This is "the system," and everyone has to live with it; be a good sport.
anklebiters	little kids who scream and snap viciously at your gaiters as you run over them on beginner slopes.
apres-ski	elaborate game played while drinking, dining, and dancing after skiing. The first player convincingly suggests a promise of delicious repayment to induce player number two to offer ascendingly expensive treats: hot chocolate and a Danish, for starters, then perhaps glogg, vodka martinis, salad bar, and steak teriyaki.

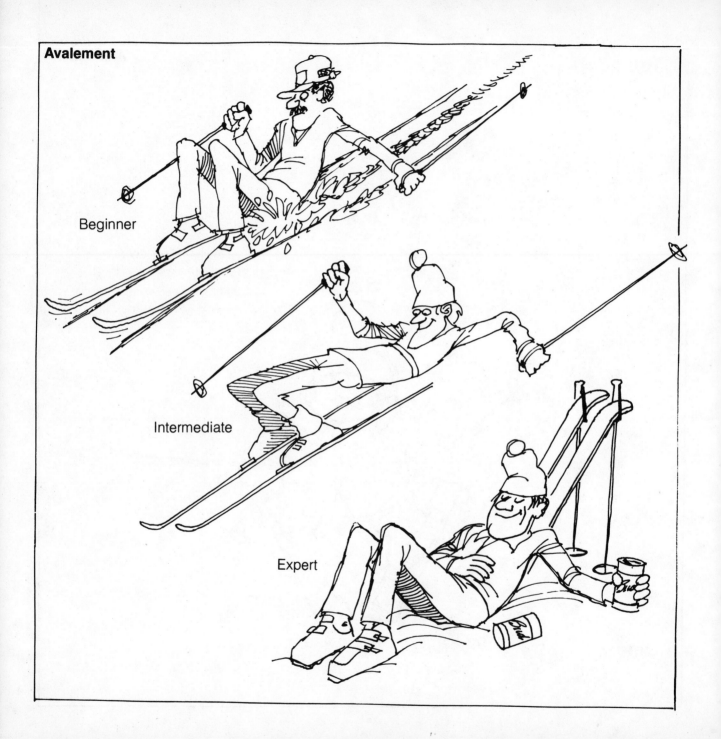

artificial snow	plasterlike substance sprayed thickly from pipe-shaped "snow guns" to create a base for skiing, simultaneously coating any passing skier's hairline, eyebrows, nostrils, ear orifices and goggles with thick goo.
Aspen	state of mind fluctuating between mild delirium and deep paranoia, accompanied by delusions of grandeur, found chiefly in residents of Pitkin County, Colorado.
Aspen-glow	warm, positive feeling brought about by eager snuffing of smelling salts or medicinal powders.
Austrians	seven million people living between the Arlberg and the plain of Hungary beyond Vienna, chosen to convey all that is good and right about skiing to the remainder of mankind with the clear understanding that this friendly, casual, protective relationship will be based on purely monetary considerations.
avalanche	phrase employed by uneducated English menials, cunningly disguised as respectable season-pass holders, while on a late-morning cruise of a day lodge, "If yew 'aven't 'ad a lanche yet, cutie, why not 'ave a lanche with me?"
avalement	technique of sitting back on the skis to get your center of gravity set for making sitzmarks.
avanti!	shout often used by an Italian skier coming down a hill at high speed to warn everyone below that he overdid the *grappa* at lunch and is in a hurry to reach the nearest restroom.
azure	1. invariant color of the sky as depicted in ski brochures 2. an important apres-ski word used to request libations. "As long azure up, get me one, too."

B

bar   location of all the best ski exploits.

bartender   helpful, parapsychiatric person who provides instant therapy to counter suicidal impulses following a very poor day on the slopes.

base   accumulation of snow, measured by a special steel measuring tape, which tends to compress considerably as it is pushed into the snow.

baskets   little round things strung on at the far end of those long thin stick-doohickies you hold in your hands. They act as "stops" to prevent the pole points from penetrating another skier far enough to do damage beyond the upper limit of your liability policy.

bassackwards   direction of a skier unwillingly descending bum-first, therefore "skiing blind" and liable to commit the regrettable *faux pas* of colliding with a large male skier.

bathtub   hole in the base created by a sizeable skier falling with considerable impetus: as the French say, when they see you heading for a fall, "Bon bathtub!"

beginner   form of ski life frequently assuming a supine or superior missionary position on the slopes.

binding   mechanism that connects boot to ski in such a way as to release after giving you a good hard twist of the ankle, just to remind you of its presence.

Boots

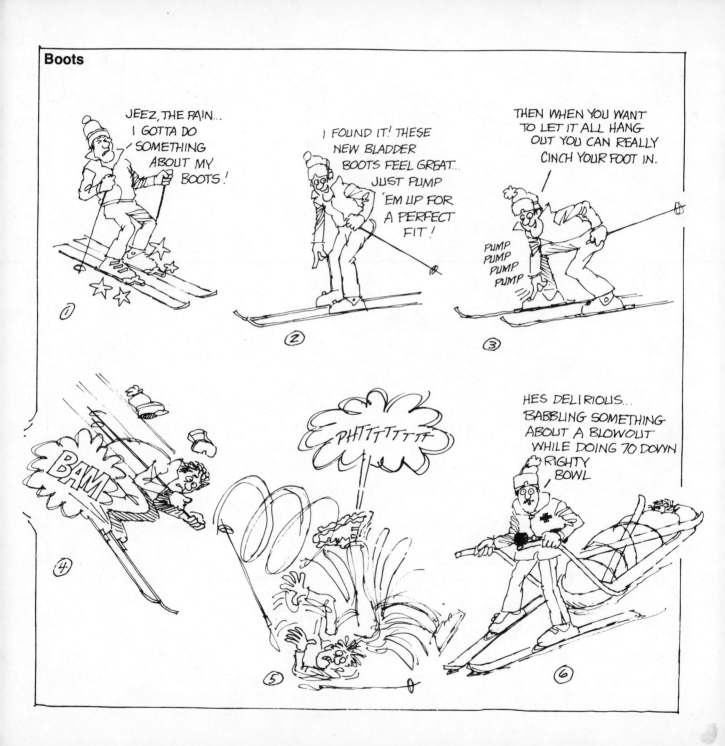

boards old-fashioned term for skis, in vogue at the same time as "Gee wilikens," "Here's mud in your eye," "Oh, boy," "That's the way the ball bounces," and other outmoded expressions.

boilerplate solid, icy surface found extensively in the East and Midwest, causing a rise in the incidence of "strawberry" contusions. Reported as "frozen granular" or, after a sufficient number of skiers have slid and scraped granules off its upper layer, as "loose granular."

Boogey late ski film star noted for his ability to portray world-weary instructors; had inimitable delivery of that searing line, "Ski it again, Sam."

boots standard skiing footwear designed to create blisters and bone spurs and considered to be the principal cause of psychopathic behavior on the slopes.

braquage turning power created by one leg leveraging its ski into a deflected position off the fulcrum provided by the other ski (as in a stem turn), or both legs simultaneously leveraging off each other's ski as fulcrums (as in a parallel turn). The word is pronounced in a deliberately mysterious manner as "bra-kwge," or "brrkge" by technically knowledgeable skiers upholding the long tradition of technical unintelligibility.

brochure playful, imaginative four-color folder depicting a resort after a snowstorm before the season opens, as well as showing expert skiers shot in other locales superimposed on its terrain; also incorporating scenic photos taken elsewhere to aid in the "artistic illusion." The text is usually studded with code, e.g., "high altitude" meaning "over 400 feet above sea level," "ample parking space" meaning "open your car door no more than two inches," and "spacious day lodge" meaning "no more crowded than Times Square on New Year's Eve."

bronze   invariable color of a ski instructor's complexion. It can be temporarily faked with "Bronzetone" or another commercial preparation, but any ski instructor is obligated to get a deep natural bronze look early in the season or face disciplinary action.

brunette   endangered species of Western female skier.

buck   American bank note: waterproof, but will shrink to half-size or less on contact with ski resort atmosphere.

buckle   to leverage shut the closures on standard ski boots, allowing delicate foot bones to press close to each other for mutual support.

C

cafeteria   any eatery with a cuisine built around the three classic cafeteria dishes: Ski and Sea (breadsticks washed down with chlorinated water from the drinking fountain), Mud and Crud (kiln-dried hamburger, smothered with the nutritious condiments found in floor sweepings), Soup and Poup (consomme-helper over a bran-and-Elmer's-Glue dumpling).

cant   wedge placed underfoot to enable a skier to edge the ski more easily or, less commendably, to ski with a stylish slant to one side, creating a fashionable appearance.

This later practice, however, permits the skier to turn only to one side and causes havoc in many situations. This is why you hear instructors ask their classes, "Can all of you turn both ways?" If anyone answers, "I cant," that student is dismissed until he "recants."

carve difficult turn requiring subtle moves which create pronounced bending of the ski. A skier's claim to have mastered this turn should be treated with the same skepticism accorded such classics as, "The check is in the mail," and "I will buy your business but I won't change it," and "Don't worry, I've had a vasectomy."

chatter 1. sound of skis skidding badly.
2. loud vibration of teeth at normal skiing temperatures.

christie skidded turn used by intermediates to slow themselves down instead of the more difficult, majestic carved turn. The christie was considered an expert turn when invented by Hannes Schneider in the twenties; today it is an act to which a noble carving skier lowers himself only as an accommodation, a gracious slowing-down so the serfs can keep up.

comma constrained position resembling the punctuation mark. Thought in the sixties to be necessary for expert technique, it led to severe lower back cramps in certain skiers. Addicts were called "commakaze."

condo short for "condominium," a group of attached dwellings individually rented to skiers for considerably more than equivalent office space on Wall Street. By bringing in some cots and standing them on end so people can sleep in the closets, and making comfy double beds out of the bathtubs, the cost per person of renting a condo can become reasonable.

cornice big overhang formed by windblown snow that can break off under a skier's weight—all too often unnecessarily designated out of bounds by the Ski Patrol, just to keep the rest of us from having fun skiing along the rim and looking over the edge, as I am doing now, seeing all the skiers far below looking so ti—

cross country insipid sort of skiing on flat terrain; the refuge of older, failed alpine skiers who have built a mystique around drudging through the pukkabush.

crud deep, mushy snow, which gives rise to cries such as "Ugh!" and "Yech!" but can be put to good use: scoop up a generous portion in a large cookie tin, store it in the refrigerator, and pat into interesting shapes to be put in guests' drinks as a charming "waste not, want not" touch for your next gala.

cruising difficult feat which involves dropping all concern with technique to just "let 'em run" down intermediate trails well within one's ability. Detractors of this philosophy have termed it "the cruisin', boozin', and snoozin' club," but, in spite of its exotic nature, cruising continues to appeal to skiers suffering from overinstruction burnout.

crust 1. thin, hard, upper layer of snow formed by melting and refreezing, which shatters as you ski on it, giving the sensation of skiing through breaking window glass. 2. quality ascribed to a skier who comes on strong the day after standing you up the evening before.

Daffy

D

daffy

aerial maneuver, accomplished by raising the tip of one ski high in front while the tail of the other ski is raised high behind, so that airborne skier is doing a split. This requires great coordination and the cooperation of a good seamstress to repair ripped pants.

day lodge

building or "hive" at the base of the mountain where skiers in constant motion ritually rub against each other's bodies in a buzzing swarm. Occasional danger of suffocation can be dealt with by instituting a vigorous shuffling, kicking motion at shin level to clear breathing space.

day ticket

permit that allows a single day's access to ski lifts. The price is arrived at by dividing the total number of American skiers into the national debt.

depth hoar

layer of round crystals that forms next to the ground, destabilizing snow layers above so that an avalanche is imminent. Invisible from the surface, depth hoar is responsible for the famous last words attributed to several members of the Ski Patrol. *I don't see no depth h—*

  o—

   a—

double chair

skiing's "Dating Game," which calls for fast, nimble word-play, backed up by quick promissory squeezes of knee and thigh. Striking the opposite player across the bridge of the nose with glove or mitten indicates a lack of interest.

down breast feathers of the eider duck sewn into "down parkas" in microscopic quantities.

downhill 1. direction resisted by beginners through grabbing other skiers and trunks of trees and digging their fingers into the snow. 2. the most risky of the trio of standard alpine races; appeals to young skiers who implicitly believe that mortality is for the aged.

downhill ski ski nearest to the bottom of the hill at the end of the turn. *Never* put your weight on this ski in a turn (no matter what the ski instructor says): putting weight on the downhill ski obviously creates imminent danger of instantly pitching down the full length of the slope.

drag any skier who skis more slowly than you do on any given day.

E

eagle aerial jump accomplished with arms and legs fully extended to the sides. This maneuver is handy for a quick "airing out" if skier is in need of a shower.

edges the outside flanges of a skier's incisor teeth, fine-honed by constant grinding due to natural anxiety over careening down slope with only a fluctuating amount of control over speed or direction.

eeee! call of a skier missing his turn on a trail bordered by mature forest.

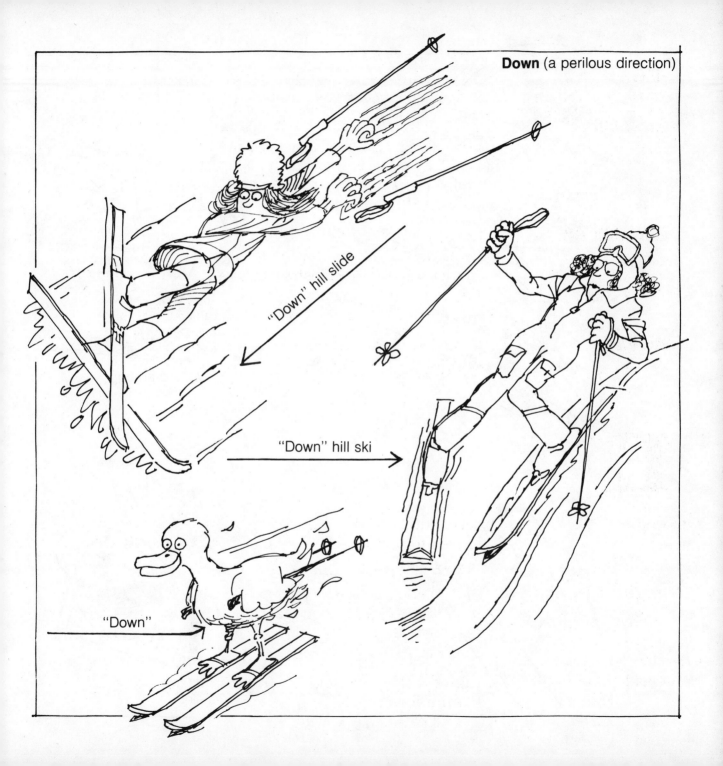

Down (a perilous direction)

"Down" hill slide

"Down" hill ski

"Down"

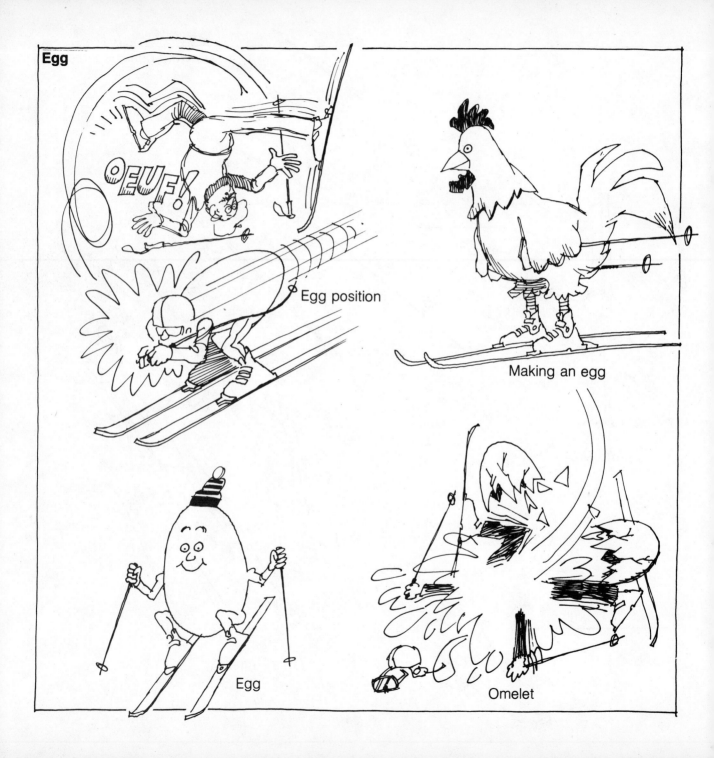

egg defensive position with head down and all else tucked in as far as it can go; for proceeding at high speed through a crowded area. Seen from the side, a human body in such a position describes an oval, or "egg," or "l'oeuf" as the French named it when they invented it as a racing maneuver. Any skier hit by an "egg" is liable to say, "Oeuf!"

elements wind, snow, cold, and other reasons for staying indoors by a fire, preferably on a bearskin rug.

equipment individual components of a complete ski outfit: includes long-lived items such as skis, which are normally good for at least two seasons, and many short-lived items such as forty-dollar gloves, which are mislaid during the third trip after purchase.

error that which other skiers do that is noticeably different from that which you do.

etiquette customs established on the slopes defining a code of behavior for most social encounters. Other skiers are always "turkeys" or "flakes," one skier never hesitates to point out another's technical faults (such as being "chicken"), knowing the other skier will value the chance to improve his ability. Whenever a skier stops, the skier behind will customarily ski slowly by holding nose with one hand and flushing an imaginary toilet with the other; the standing skier will reply with a "stickfinger salute" (a pumping of the fist with middle finger extended). A skier seeking to join an already-formed group must request permission by asking, "Want to watch a real skier?" He will be ritually answered, "Sure. Keep checking for tears in the back of our pants, will you?" Slow skiers in a group must never be allowed to rest; as soon as they catch up, the others of the party must ski away. Literally thousands of such customs form a rich "skiing social fabric," the complexity and subtlety of which can only be suggested here.

extension	reflexive elongation of one's body accompanying first sight of a humongous dropoff on a trail that was supposed to be a piece of cake.
external turning forces	forces other than the skier's own muscular exertion that effect a change of direction: collisions with other skiers, glancing blows from passing grooming vehicles, or the sudden sight of one's mate down the slope just after one has befriended a charming person newly met on the chairlift.
extreme	description of terrain where a single fall or missed turn is likely to be the last one you will ever make—and why did you let yourself get talked into coming up here in the first place?

F

fall	sincere attempt to slow down.
fall line	narrow furrow straight downhill made by nose of skier in a forward fall.
fanny pack	bustle-shaped, belted carryall favored by female skiers —named after the original worn at St. Moritz by Fanny Hill.

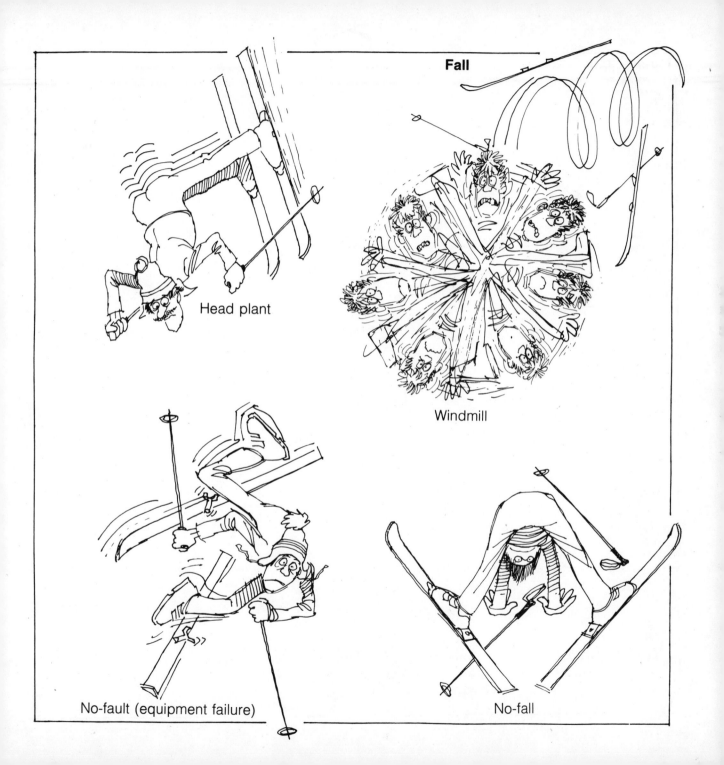

Fall

Head plant

Windmill

No-fault (equipment failure)

No-fall

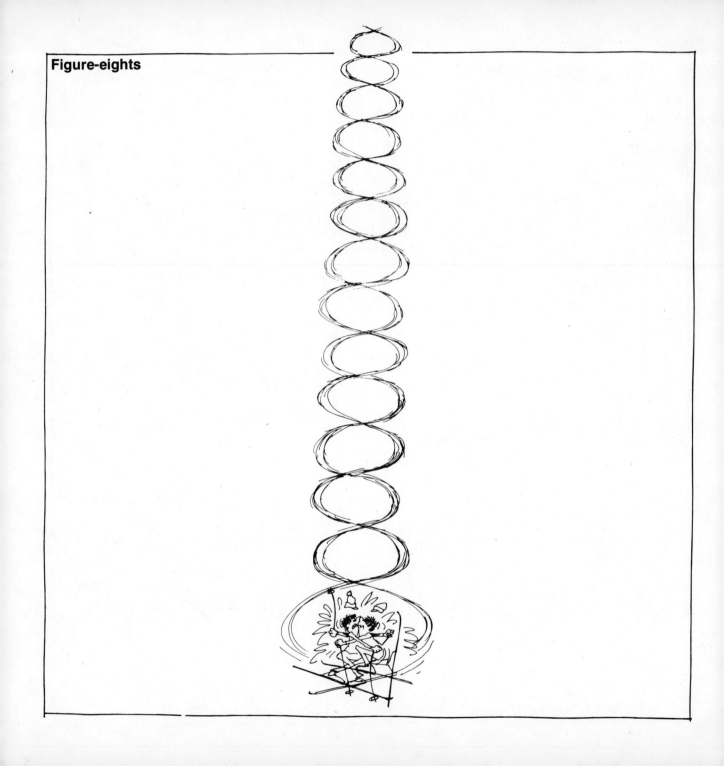

fear of steeps mental state characterized by spasmodic legs, rigor mortis grip on poles, icy stomach pit, and sniveling sounds issuing from the larynx. There is no known cure for this affliction.

figure-eights tracks left by a duo of skiers making exactly opposite turns and trying desperately to avoid hitting each other as they cross closer and closer on every turn.

FIS *abbr. Federation International de Ski*, the amateur racing union. It ensures that amateurs' wages, endorsements, and under-the-table emoluments are never exceeded by those of professional racers.

flex bending characteristics of a ski, rated by resting tail and tip of the ski on chairs set five feet apart and seating skiers on midsection of ski. The *flex rating* of the ski is the number of skiers it takes to make the middle of the ski bend down and touch the floor.

flexion momentary compaction of legs that gets skier through, with minimum chance of injury, a group of skiers blocking a trail or an inadvertent collision with the lift line.

flush 1. a series of race flags set one after the other down the fall line. 2. moves executed by a group of skiers attempting to lose one of their party deemed undesirable. See *drag*.

freestyle 1. three-part discipline of style competition in ballet, moguls, and aerials. 2. abandonment of more formal technique when plummeting into a ravine.

fun universal adjective describing the sport of skiing in all magazines, advertisements, and brochures. Any skier knows that it's not all that easy to reach the ideal situation where one does have fun, the weather being untrustworthy, the skis likewise unreliable, and even the old physique sometimes giving one trouble; therefore, it makes sense to "plan for fun" *after* skiing, when one has control of the thermostat and the key to the liquor cabinet as well as the opportunity to invite any number of interesting people to join in the festivities.

fundamentals boring, repetitive moves instructors claim a skier has to learn to make automatically in order to enjoy skiing. Well, many skiers who have just never taken a lesson are out there right now, thundering down the slopes and getting a lot of attention from everyone. Fundamentals are overrated, obviously.

G

gelandesprung anything "sprung for" by another as in, "Good old George, he gelandesprung for the whole dinner check."

giant slalom! 1. traditional, hearty salutation given to an Israeli skier who is lying supine after having cleanly broken *both* poles of his last gate. 2. alpine race through flags involving higher speed and fewer gates than slalom; an event dominated by racers having polished techniques and large tax-free municipal bond investments.

glade trail cut with some trees left standing, based on the theory that skiers enjoy the challenge.

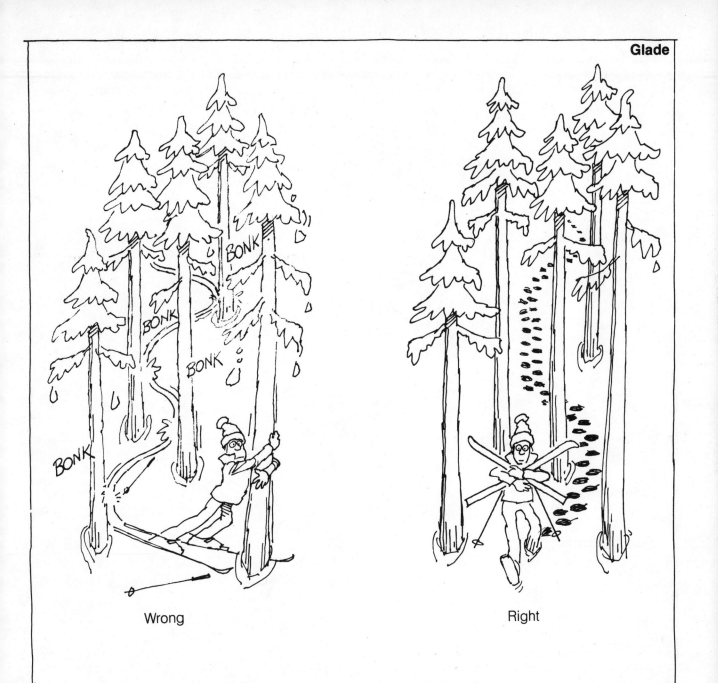

Wrong

Right

Gravity

goggles   pair of lenses suspended in a frame in front of a skier's eyes designed to fog completely at the appearance of any impending danger.

gondola   lift passenger car that offers an unusual amount of privacy by comparison with conveyances on other lifts. Cars are usually posted with an advisory on local conditions affecting any contemplated action during the ride —for example, "This gondola is a compact model; the maximum ride is twelve minutes and there are persistent drafts through the cracks. Only small, agile skiers with a high metabolism, therefore, will be able to fully engage in and enjoy the unique camaraderie of the complete gondola experience."

gorilla   1. nickname for modern "wide track" ski stance, giving skiers the look of being crotchbound and afflicted with permanent stomach cramps—a poor substitute for the graceful, classic legs-together stance popularized by Stein Eriksen in the fifties. 2. name applied to any member of the Ski Patrol who interferes with the skier's God-given right to go as fast as he or she pleases.

gravity   fateful force that pulls the skier straight downhill in spite of feeble efforts to turn to one side or the other. The "law of gravity" was repealed by the Colorado state legislature in 1972—a move aimed at boosting winter tourism by eliminating the need for lifts. The repeal was rescinded in an ultimately unsuccessful attempt to bring the '76 Olympics to the state. Currently, gravity is still in effect in Colorado.

grooming vehicles converted grain harvesters that are raced daily to the top of the mountain by macho drivers to see who can get there first (allegedly to improve the quality of snow); drivers get additional race points for any skiers shunted into the woods on the way up.

gully! mild expression of surprise at finding oneself airborne over a forty-foot drop.

H

Hannes Schneider ghost of the historic figure who invented the Arlberg technique, said to hover above St. Anton after hours near the Krazy Kangaruh.

headwall long, nearly vertical drop ranging from a foot and a half in the Midwest to 1000 feet at Tuckerman's Ravine, New Hampshire.

heel thrust grinding motion of an instructor's foot to put out a last cigarette before facing class.

herringbone 1. *n.* prestigious weave for tweed stretch pants. 2. *v.* to climb back up the trail hastily in an awkward attempt to retrieve a lost hat.

holding 1. illegal move in the lift line game. 2. the highly unusual state wherein a ski mysteriously goes in the direction it is pointed.

hot dog male skier.

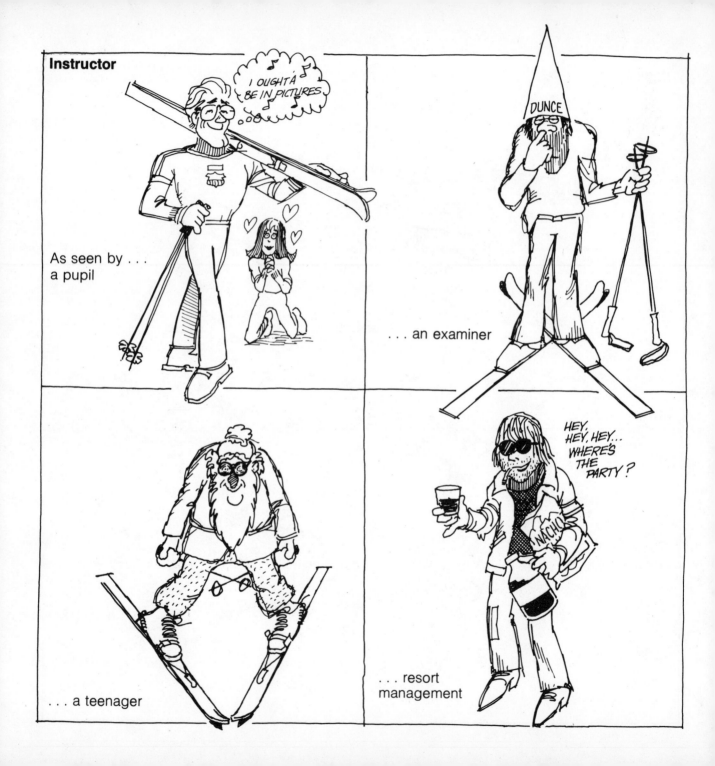

I

ice   hard surface reckoned to be the best acceleration device in the sport, with gradations from *white* through *green* to *blue*: skiers hitting white ice will slide not more than a hundred yards or so; skiers hitting green ice can count on coming to a stop somewhere between the bottom lift terminal and the base lodge; skiers hitting blue ice should wear crash helmets and body pads to reduce possible injuries sustained when blasting through both walls of the cafeteria and coming to a hard stop against a car in the parking lot beyond.

inexplicable   description of a fall taken by oneself when other skiers are too remote to have been at fault.

infinite   1. size of the novice slope. 2. distance between the top and the bottom of the ramp at the upper end of the chair lift.

inside ski   safe ski to rest weight on when going around a turn; allows skier to keep center of gravity near the snow, the better to initiate body braking at the finish.

instructor   catlike creature with compulsory tan, wearing mirrored sunglasses; most at ease with humans of opposite sex; can be flushed out of instructor's shack and forced to give lessons by threatening deprivation of resort-supplied caffeine ration; can say, "Hello, I am your ski instructor" in mechanical tones, but lacks responsiveness unless offered lunch or apres-ski entertainment.

intermarriage	nuptials between an expert skier and an intermediate or a beginner.

J

jargon	language used by a ski instructor to address his class when he doesn't want the students to know what he is saying. See *jive*.
jaundiced	description of a skier whose carefully coordinated outfit is effortlessly outclassed by that of another member of the group.
jaunt	any cross-country tour of fifty miles or less, and requiring packs of no more than fifty pounds.
jet turn	complex expert turn which a competent skier may have been undertaking when he fell backward into an instructor's class.
jigger	thingamabob used to close the what-cha-call-it around there by the, uh, backside of the boot.
jive	ski instructor's language used when the instructor wants the class to think they understand him.
Joan of Arc	female member of the party who voluntarily leaves the slopes early to buy groceries and start the potatoes.
jolt	realization that one's spouse is learning much faster in ski class than oneself.

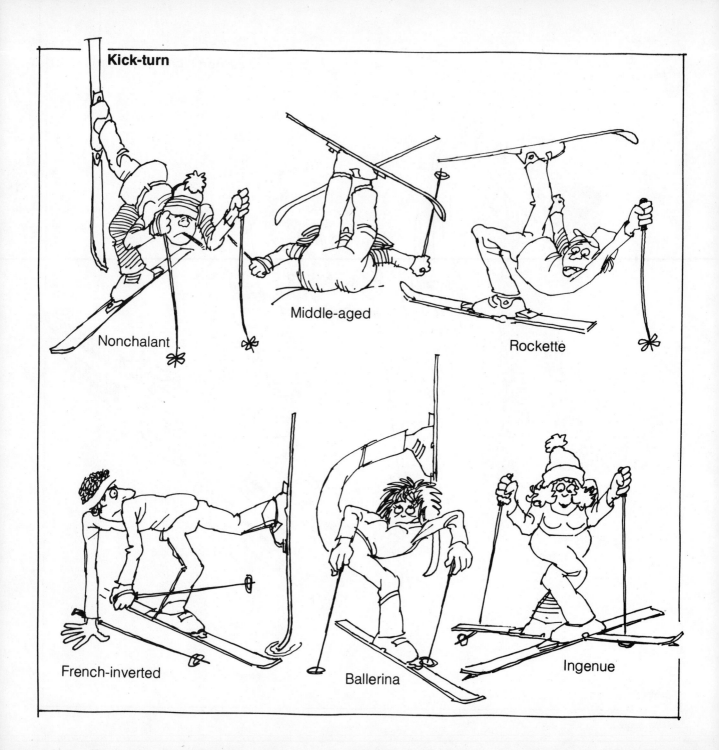

Kick-turn

Nonchalant

Middle-aged

Rockette

French-inverted

Ballerina

Ingenue

Judas

male skier leaving the slopes with a "Joan of Arc," harboring devious intentions, resulting in a late dinner for everyone.

jump

maneuver performed to clear the body of a skier lying prone on the trail around a blind corner.

jumpsuit

one-piece ski suit. The answer of the clothing manufacturers to the threat posed by jeans: you buy the jacket, you buy the pants.

junk

"mashed potatoes"; the deep, soft, gooey, hard-to-ski snow; can be frozen and served sprinkled with paprika.

juvenile

term used to describe antics of other skiers when you have a hangover.

kannonen

Ger: cannon; any loudmouthed skier.

ketchup

vitamin supplement used by part-time resort employees.

kick turn

standing maneuver to accomplish an about-face. To execute: stand facing side of slope; kick the downhill ski up on its tail, and then swing it slowly around so it points 180 degrees in the opposite direction; you are now in the painful *plié* position from which you can extricate yourself by calling on any nearby skier to help you pull the other ski around.

knee crank	any skier who persistently taps his kneecap, listens for loose cartilage, wraps it in an Ace bandage, etc.
kneissl!	sound made by a sneezing Austrian.
knickers	standard cross-country pants, resembling Victorian "bloomers," eminently practical garments discarded by anyone with the money to buy one of those new slick one-piece racing suits.
krypton	what Superman's skis are made of.

L

langlauf	*Ger*: winner of a cross-country race; literally, "He who laughs last laughs longest."
lang unterwasche	*Ger*: long underwear; literally, "a long time between washings."
lateral	immediate area on both sides of the skier, which can be kept clear by vigorously swinging the ski poles to and fro at full arm's length.
lateral projection	a leap to the side to avoid an immovable object, keenly reminding the skier of his mortality.
lean	vital concept in ski technique. *Lean away* from whatever seems to be the danger in the situation. For example, when heading downhill, *lean back*, away from the steep part in front of you. When turning, *lean uphill* by all means (you don't really want to lean downhill and

The new cross-country gear   The new downhill gear

fall all the way to the bottom, do you?). Furthermore, *lean toward* the center of the trail whenever you head for the edge. Follow these simple rules and you will always be solidly grounded in the sport.

lederhosen	kinky leather shorts.
lift attendants	locals, often handsomely outfitted in resort-supplied uniforms. It might pay to occasionally offer small courtesies to attendants, as such people can take "underdog's revenge" by holding a chair too long, so it smashes leg tendons or calf muscles in a crippling manner. Attendants can also retract chair slightly as the skier sits on it, causing ski tips to dip and catch in snow as the chair takes off, pulling the skier headfirst out of the chair onto the snow.
lift line	a game with a list of allowable gambits, such as walking your skis across the tails of the skier ahead so he is immobilized until you can get the inside lane on the corner; waving to some skiers in front as if they were friends, then skiing up to start a conversation while insinuating yourself into the line ten places ahead; stumbling and "accidentally" jamming a knee in your neighbor's thigh to sneak in ahead of him when he doubles up in pain. Not allowable: outright grappling or penetration of another skier with the point of your pole.
line	racer's particular plan of attack on a given course, which he must memorize so that, as he reaches any given gate, he can react according to plan and increase the number of gates he takes standing before the inevitable blowout.
lip	most powerful muscle in some skiers' bodies.

lodge   type of accommodations (varying from spartan to luxurious) wherein much apres-ski activity is proposed and some occasionally consummated. Thoughtful architectural planning of interconnecting balconies and shared bathrooms facilitates this. Beware of inns with pseudo-Bavarian names whose architecture may well reflect a pervading Germanic attitude that one is here simply to ski.

longthong   medieval ski binding, which was wetted, bound around and around the boot, and tied to the ski. As the leather dried, it slowly shrank until the foot was put under the same highly effective pressure that is produced today by buckle closures.

M

macadam   smooth tar layer that is a major feature of modern resorts; covers unsightly primitive grass meadows, prepares area for auto parking, fast-food restaurants, etc.

map   representation on paper of the ski resort terrain, supplied free to skiers, printed in type too small to be read except under studio light and on paper that self-destructs when damp.

master plan   architectural plan of a projected resort to be implemented when rich investors show up; modified to a

great extent by blindly selling off property when rich investors fail to show up.

method	approach of a particular school of instruction, which precludes consideration of any other. Many skiers opt for the Malarky method, enunciated by the famous Irish skier, J. Malarky, to wit, "Whenever I feel like improving my ski technique, I lie down until the feeling goes away."
mezzo giro su se stresso	*Ital*: kick turn; literally, "You want me to do what?"
missile	beginner.
mitten	covering worn to protect hands by those who do not understand that gloves are compulsory. See *turkey*.
mitten cover	protective covering worn to prevent chafing from icy rope tows in the very different and hardly recognizable sub-arctic version of the sport practiced in the Midwest.
Moebius Flip	inverted aerial in which the skier literally turns himself inside out and then reverses the procedure halfway through to land intact.
mogul event	freestyle event consisting of skiing a high-speed run with trick jumps over big moguls without mashing kneecap into nose more than once or twice.
moguls	1. key word used by Southern male skiers seeking companionship on the slopes, "We need mo' guls!" 2. *archaic*: bumps appearing on the slopes before the days of grooming machines.
mountain	wasteland of rock, brush, trees, birds, and wild animals going unused before the arrival of the ski resort.

N

natural	the kind of skiing taught here, as opposed to elsewhere.
Neissl	Austrian-made short ski.
nippy	windchill factor of minus 50° or so (in New England).
noodle ski	ski with a squishy layer of well-done noodles at the core; features spineless, torqueless construction, built for extremely bumpy terrain. Its design qualities are often mimicked by conventional skis used more than three seasons.
nooner	preview of apres-ski.

O

open racing	nefarious scheme for letting pro racers get their hands on money intended for amateurs.
orienteering	formal game that involves finding one's way through unknown woods on skis in the dead of winter with compass and map. The game is slowly dying out through attrition of players due to their failure to find their way through unknown woods in the dead of winter on skis with compass and map.
orthopedics	branch of medicine for reconstituting displaced bones and joints; keeps the sport of skiing alive, and vice versa.

outlaw	instructor who teaches "underground," without giving the ski school its cut. He usually fails to understand the necessity for keeping instruction boring.
outrigger	freestyle turn executed with one ski extended low and to the side like an outrigger of a canoe; handy for clearing a freestyler's favorite trails of unwanted skiers.
out of bounds	roped-off terrain posted with warnings generally pooh-poohed by adventuresome skiers who ski through ropes and signs without telling anyone, so that sometimes no one finds out they did it until Spring.
overedge	to tilt a ski so much on edge that it cuts through the base to the grass, causing much embarrassment to the management of a ski resort.

P

P-turn	sharp turn into the woods to make a phone call.
pacifier	small object held in the mouth, known as the "poor man's pacemaker," which can be helpful in keeping calm while skiing tricky terrain.
packed powder	misnomer often used in ski reports. It's really "packed loose snow" since powder has to be, by definition, definitely unpacked—but you have to admit that "powder" does sound ever so much nicer.
panic	normal state of a skier's mind when nothing unusual is happening.

parallel	advanced technique of skiing whereby the tips and tails of skis are kept the same distance apart. If you can do it, you are okay; skiers who cannot ski parallel are not okay.
paraski race	event in which skiers jump from a plane and parachute accurately onto a small target on a ski slope, put on skis, and race into a tree.
parenthesis	bow-legged skier badly in need of canting.
parka	ski jacket; derived from the New England word "parker," a jacket suitable for necking in the car in winter.
Peoria	Illinois town to which all ski resort marketing departments pitch their advertising.
peripheral vision	the most useful thing to have on the slopes, next to a suit of armor.
piste	*Fr*: trail; colloquially: a feeling of disgust at one's own poor performance on skis.
plow	form of descent with ski tips together and tails apart. This stance allows an unsure skier to brake without turning, even if the skier's knees are shaking and eyes watering.
pole	long, sharp hand-held instrument used for fending off other skiers; also useful for scaring off cars coming too close in the parking lot. Unfortunately, on the slope, poles are worse than useless: one or the other is constantly getting caught under the skis, causing the skier to stumble; or between the legs, tripping the skier up; or sticking point-first in the snow, jamming the handle into the skier's midsection or pulling him off balance to

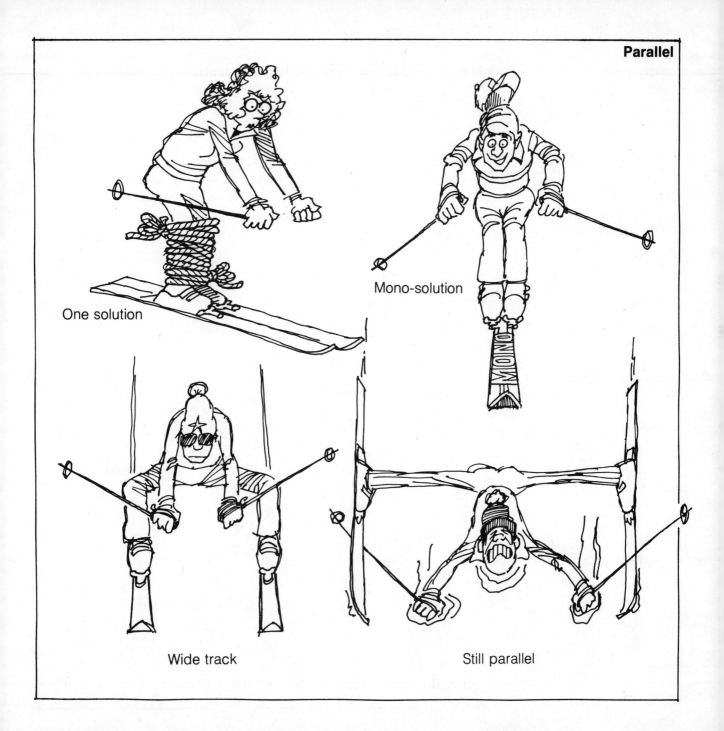

One solution

Mono-solution

Wide track

Still parallel

one side. If only ski resorts were properly supportive, they would let skiers send their poles down with the chair lift each time, so they could be picked up again at the bottom. This would allow skiers to retain the use of their poles for defensive purposes in the lift line and around the base lodge, yet save them the bother of the poles on the slopes.

pole plant	skinny, hardy perennial that can serve as support for ivy and tomato vines. Simply plant old broken poles in tamped dirt and water every other day; produces small "basket" blooms in Spring.
powder	light, fluffy snow; creates desirable conditions which occur immediately before your vacation at the resort.
powder skis	any stiff skis that will plane to the surface, just like water skis; soft skis will only curl up at the tips in powder and throw you over backward!
powder technique	1. repeat the Lord's Prayer. 2. repeat any other invocation coming to mind. 3. pick up an old U.S. Army Tenth Mountain Division ski manual and turn to instructions for a standing kick turn. As you can see, all you have to do is traverse to one side of trail, kick skis around, traverse back to other side, etc. Pretty soon you'll have made it all the way down to the bottom—a real powder skier!
prejump	hop off the side of the trail into the woods preceding the removal of skis, in order to walk down beside a steep, dangerous stretch.
private lesson	punishment given to out-of-favor instructors.

Q

quality universal reason given for raising lift prices.

quersprung aborted jump turn in which one ski goes right, the other one left, and the skier into a forward roll. It is very amusing to watch when done inadvertently by some hot shot.

quintillion total number of snowflakes in a handful, usually lodged somewhere down around the bottom of the spinal column.

R

racer species of skier enjoying terrain only when it has been planted with festive flags. Racing requires such complete dedication that, on retirement, racers must undergo retraining in the English language and conventional social behavior.

racer burnout condition in which every square inch of a racer's uniform is taken up by a sponsor's decal or patch. In this case, the racer is said to be "burned out."

railed bottom 1. bottom of a ski after the soft P-tex base has worn down, leaving the edges higher, like rails. 2. bottom of a skier after a sitting fall onto the backs of the skis.

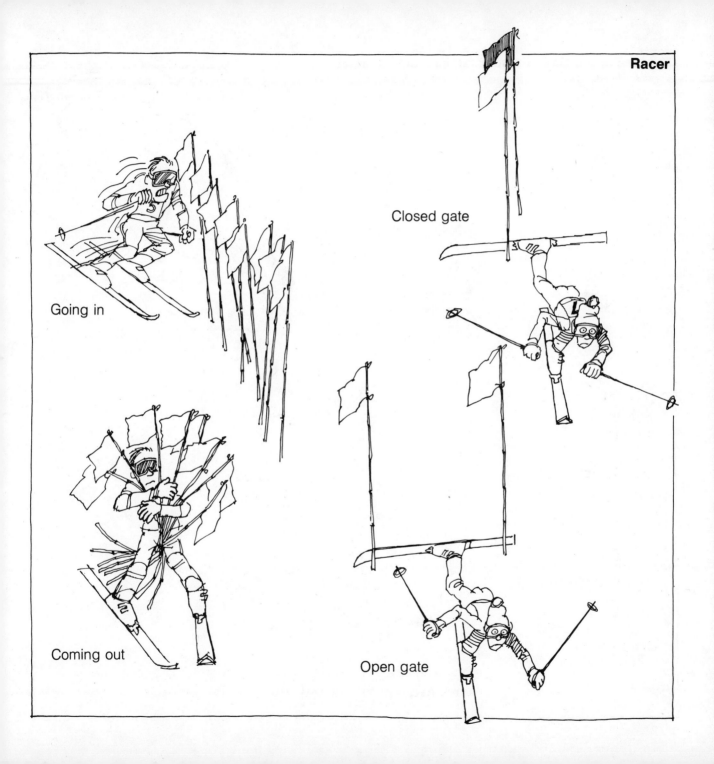

Going in

Coming out

Closed gate

Open gate

Rapture of the Deep Powder (an incurable madness)

rapture of the deep powder	dangerous mental state that strikes a skier after experiencing a good run down a long slope of hip-deep white stuff; a feeling of flying or being "high" that may take days to subside. Some victims never "come down" at all: the only known cure is "cold turkey," three consecutive weeks of skiing in Ohio.
release binding	rigid device which attaches boot to ski and detaches after a certain amount of painful twisting; invented in the Fifties by Hjalmar Hvam, whose sales motto was "Hvoom with Hvam," implying a pain-free departure from the skis—a hvast exaggeration.
reploiement	namby-pamby way of skiing moguls with "soft legs" instead of stiff-legging them.
resort	ski area with indoor toilets.
retention strap	means for holding skis in proximity of boots after the binding releases; largely replaced today by ski brakes, because straps make skis windmill, beating up an embarrassing, frothy wake of "Rediwhip" behind the sliding skier.
retraction	speech made after spraying snow on a considerably bigger skier than oneself.
reverse camber	1. particular construction of a ski which makes ski soft enough to turn up at both ends under skier's weight. 2. condition of brand-new skis after a season's use by a teenager.
rock skis	special type of skis worn when listening to an album by Heavy Metal on one's Walkman.

roll	clever way to end a turn.
rope tow	wet, icy line strung uphill in an endless loop between a drive wheel on the bottom and a pulley wheel on the top. By grasping the rope, you can easily: 1. get a refreshing facial spray as the sopping wet rope whizzes through your mittens. 2. get pulled all the way to the top even though you fall immediately after you start (just "hold on tight" and you will get there). 3. freeze to the line so that, as the rope rises higher and higher off the snow, you get a wonderful aerial ride, hanging by your thumbs!
royal christie	turn made with one ski purposely held aloft to make ordinary skiers feel inadequate.
ruade	*Fr*: an offensive manuever: tails of skis are kicked upward, showering snow in the face of a nearby, unsuspecting wimp.
rucklage	*Ger*: to lean back on the skis; a sensible way of dealing with a steep slope.
Rules of the Road	precepts that regulate ski traffic for safety, as follows: 1. first skier at an intersection gets blindsided by the second skier. 2. four skiers standing in a group in the middle of a narrow trail can force all others to shave the trees to go around them. 3. overtaking skier screams "Track!" in an hysterical voice right behind the skier being overtaken, and gets points if the overtaken skier flinches. 4. when two skiers converge simultaneously at an intersection, the heavier, faster skier flattens the lighter, slower skier. 5. skier stops short above another, showers snow on him, and assumes a sneering expression.

Schuss

run multipurpose word: 1. *v.* to descend with skis. 2. *n.* a particular track on a slope laid out for the skier. 3. *n.* a warning shout by a friend when he notices that a) the owner of the brand-new poles you "temporarily borrowed" has spotted you in the lift line and b) he is six feet tall and plays football for Notre Dame.

S

schmertz sharp pang produced by the sound of a ski striking a rock after a two-hour tuning job.

schuss to gun down the fall line in an excess of passion, spurred on by the taste of the forbidden fruit of high speed. Such behavior is a frequent indicator of severe "schussederasty," a very serious perversion in which speed is substituted for sex. The disease is considered incurable.

short skis attention-getters used by skiers who are unable to attract notice through expertise; also often used by "permanent intermediates" to enable them to descend expert slopes, where they catastrophically create short, choppy moguls that spoil the skiing. Vigilante groups of good skiers have formed to seize short skis—whenever and wherever found—off ski racks, car racks, and the like, to be sold to condo owners as doorstops or fireplace kindling.

side roll complicated freestyle trick: a highly trained performer drops downhill on his speeding skis with head tucked in and swings skis overhead in a shoulder roll, laying skis down again in position for his standing recovery. The ordinary skier's version of this is termed "a fall."

sitzmark shallow depression occasioned by impact of the rear of a skier sliding on snow; cumulatively, sitzmarks provide an effective excuse for standing up and drinking rather than sitting down and eating.

skare *Nor*: breakable crust; a perilous condition that is skary as hell.

ski area actual slopes of a resort, displaying a magnificent variety of terrain and scenery, whose true attractions can be sufficiently appreciated only by reading about them in the brochure.

ski brake spring-loaded prong on the ski binding that quickly pins a loose ski to the snow. Its widespread use has all but eliminated the fun of screaming "Ski! Ski!" as in the good old days when a loose ski would call for a hot pursuit that ended only when some brave soul would trap the ski by stepping on it, eliciting general applause from onlookers. Skiing just ain't the fun it used to be.

ski bum sore hindquarters caused by repeated backward falls; a necessary penalty for the fun of creating *sitzmarks* and *bathtubs*.

ski fever wild, midsummer mental state in which a skier exhumes old copies of ski magazines, reads the letter columns, and then frequents ski shops, ignoring the skateboards and buying a third and fourth edge sharpener, extra rubber ski straps, and packs of high-altitude razor blades.

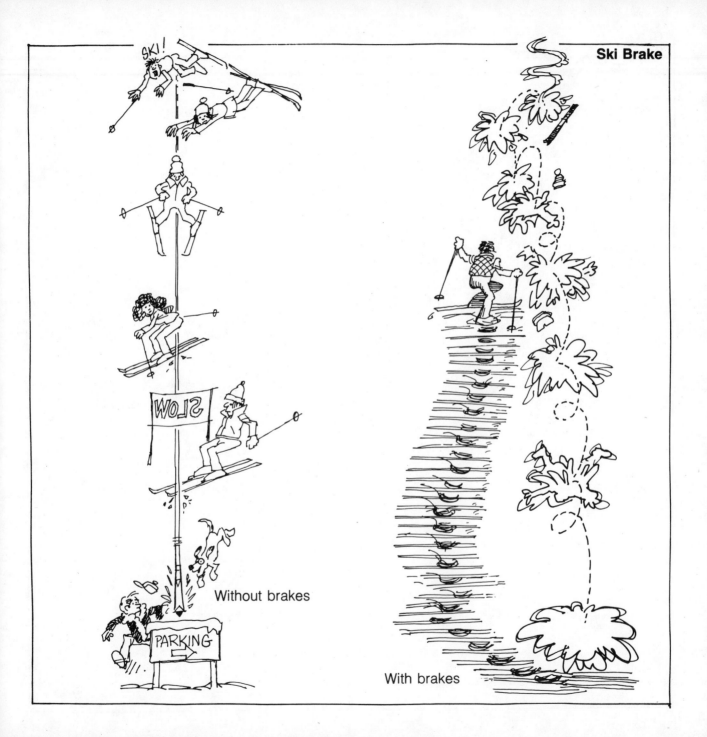

Ski Brake

Without brakes

With brakes

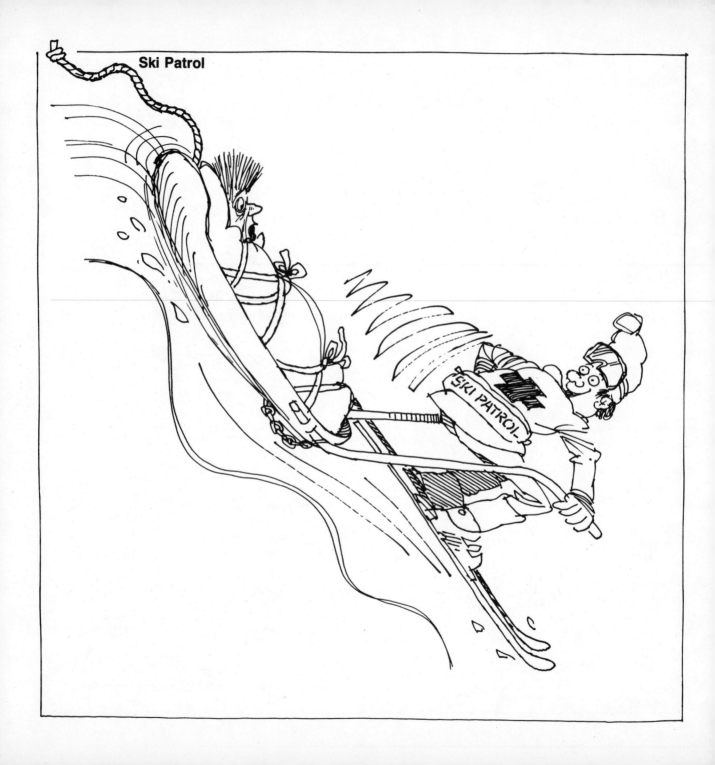

Ski Patrol	rag-tag collection of individuals who clear the slopes of fallen skiers blocking the trail.
ski report	dissemination of information about snow conditions through the use of codes: "several inches of new powder" means "a passing cloud lightly dusted the slab, crust, and rock of the upper mountain"; "frozen granular" is code telling the management's immediate family and friends to stay away from the area until further notice; "five to ten inches of new snow" means "as measured in the drift that piles up behind Harry's cabin in the woods."
ski rites	ceremonies occurring after a ski has snapped in two at the end of a long and useful life. The ski is wrapped in an old scarf and laid to rest in an untouched snowdrift while the friends of the owner intone the words of the Ski Service, "Thy mountains are so large, and this ski so small . . .," making everyone feel good for having "gone through it" rather than taking it out on the lift attendants.
ski school meeting place	area where ski instructors assemble for the purpose of being parcelled out to students, a process known among instructors as "feeding the sharks."
skins	strips of nylon hair fastened to ski bottoms, which allow skiers to climb directly uphill on alpine skis. Skins are made to adhere to skis by means of a laborious process in which a messy goo is painted on and "cured" by hanging skins over a stove before being stuck onto skis —a lengthy, finicky process enabling the skier to realize how inexpensive helicopters really are.

skis   long, narrow planklike objects attached to each foot for the purpose of going forward and backward over snow. They give a great deal of trouble to skiers by insisting on heading for large, hard objects such as maintenance sheds. All skis are identical except for length and are all manufactured in a secret location in Austria, given different cosmetics, and then shipped to brand-name owners all over the world to be sold at prices which differ according to the advertising budget of the brand.

slalom   most common form of alpine racing; the winning skier is the one figuring out which flag goes with what gate.

snowplow   technique that traditionally served as a rite of passage from nonskier to skier and that required steel hamstrings, sprung hip sockets, and immense quads; it has now been replaced by the less rigorous "wedge," which any creampuff can do.

Snowmass   elaborate prayer intoned by Catholic or Episcopal skiers asking for more snow during the coming week.

snowsnake   person met on a chairlift who fails to show up at the cafeteria at noon as promised.

spiral   fracture line that winds round and round the tibia; calls for a cast-signing party.

split   partial course time given in cross-country races to each racer along the way, together with the times of his chief rivals and reminders of how many endorsements are riding on this one.

spring skiing   late-season skiing conditions when the frustrations of a hard season disappear in a mellow glow of accom-

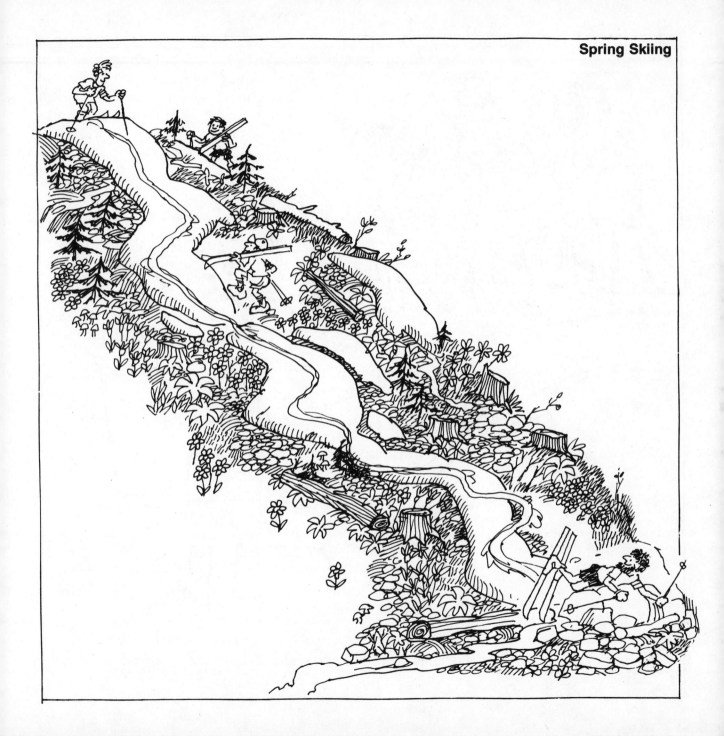

plishment, as skis whizz through snow softened by an occasional drizzle. Nonetheless, the skier's happiness is tinged with a certain sadness at the imminent demise of the season and, along with that, the imminent demise of the skis, which encounter more and more rock and dirt as the snow melts down faster and faster.

starter ski kit ski parts sold separately with instructions for assembly: materials include two rolls of four-inch fiberglass cloth, a gallon of epoxy, two seven-foot strips of P-tex and matching ribbons of steel edge, a bucket of pine chips, and a jumbo bottle of Elmer's Glue. Costs $50 to $60. For another hundred, the manufacturer will glue the chips into a core—all you have to do is lay the fiberglass on to produce the proper ski shape, add the bottoms and edges, and apply the cosmetics. (For another hundred or so, the manufacturer will do the whole job for you, which gives you time to build your own chairlift right in your backyard: kits start at $40,000 and include ten steel lift-tower assemblies, eighty chairs, and cable-weaving gear.)

steilhang sudden drop steep enough to hang a skier's style — or steil — up.

stem colloquial: the leg of a comely female skier; *stemmer*: a lady with good-looking legs; *all stemmed up*: bodily condition of a male looking at a stemmer; *stem turn*: a comely female does a turnabout and reprimands overt ogler; *stemming*: overt ogling.

student ski school enrollee not necessarily willing to ski except to placate friends and family who have brought him or her to the resort at a great deal of expense.

Swiss group of people owning a large part of Europe's post-card real estate and commonly exhibiting great ingenuity in renting parts of its steep portions at equally steep prices to tourists with numbered bank accounts in Zurich.

T

T-bar companionable form of lift that drags two skiers over snow, side by side, leaving the arm nearest the other skier free for exploratory moves.

TC *abbr.* Terror Crouch, a beginner's involuntary squatting position, from which he can only be extricated after he learns to relax and enjoy his low profile.

technique ability to explain convincingly to a person just met in the cafeteria line that one has been suddenly and fatally attracted: possessed to marked degree by most ski instructors.

Tenth Mountain United States Army division in World War II, trained extensively for combat on skis and shipped to Italy. While the outfit never did get to use their skis, they did drive the Germans northward on foot until they surrendered with their backs against the Alps. The returning Tenth brought all their unused equipment back, flooding America with cheap skis, boots, and poles — and interminable war stories. "Tenth Mountain skis" have long since disappeared, but the telling of Tenth Mountain stories goes on. "Old ski soldiers never die, they just drone away . . . ," as the saying goes.

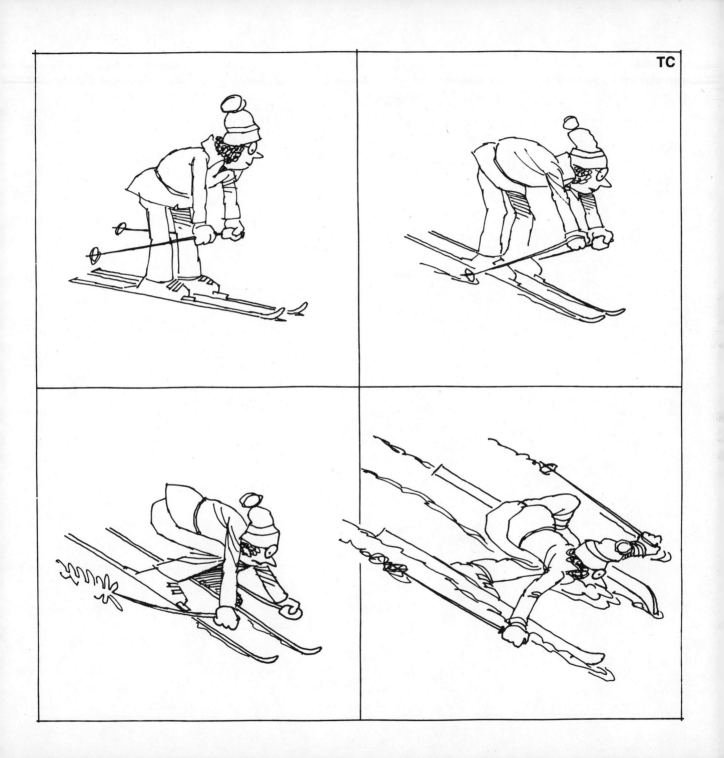

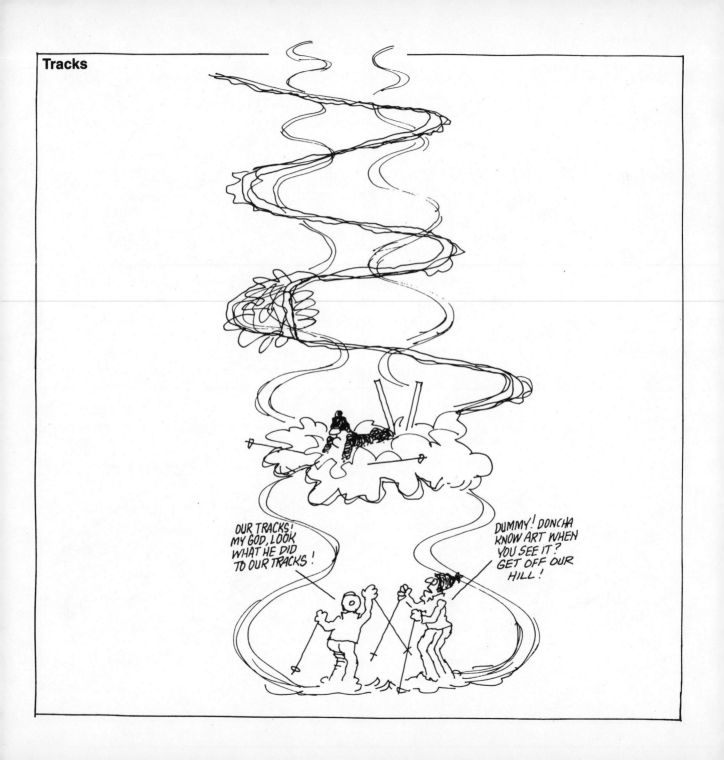

tip	part of a ski pointing in the direction the skier does not wish to go.
tip cross	ski tip unhappy after being crushed under the other tip and skier's chest, in that order.
toboggan	type of transportation operated by the Ski Patrol. Toboggan patrolman should be picked carefully: if the "driver" loses control, the toboggan accelerates like crazy until it hits something!
touring	short for "cross-country touring," a contemplative, noncompetitive form of skiing in which one takes a leisurely trip and tries to get back to the starting point sooner than anyone else.
tourist	nonlocal skier, not a sharp dresser, has a tendency to maintain a firm belief in resort advertising and the Tooth Fairy.
track	visible "signature" of a skier, ranging in cursive skill from illiterate zigzags to expert arabesques prized as trophies of skill and elan—before being obliterated by the herd.
trail	larger or smaller opening in surrounding forest. Always remember: some trails may have rocks, stumps, and pits right under the snow—let someone else make first track!
transition	sudden flattening of terrain at the end of a steep which produces a G force on the skier that grows to huge proportions, enabling skier to test the ability of the "quads" and other leg muscles to prevent the chin from touching the knees.

traverse	to ski across (rather than down) the slope; it is the only direction not requiring stressful turning or stopping maneuvers. Unfortunately, a traverse does not lead toward the bottom, but it's nice to get a rest.
tuck	racing position for a downhill event, which can involve speed sup to sixty miles an hour: head down, back level, and hands ahead—normally accompanied by slow intonation of vowels: *Aaaaah, ooooups, ohhhhhhuh! ughhh, eeeeesus! arrghh! owwww! Yiiiii . . .*
tuning	outlet for a secret childish delight in having bits of high-carbon steel and P-tex shavings embedded in one's cuticles on the pretext of filing skis to improve their performance.
tuque	heavy wool stocking cap worn by French-speaking skiers in Quebec. If you happen to be there, playfully snatch one from a native's head. You then have a chance to shout, *"Ah, monsieur, I have tuque your tuque!"*
turkey	tourist who does not know how to dress, let alone ski. He therefore deserves to hear rude gobbling noises made by locals as he passes by.
turn	maneuver performed by advanced skiers employing semi-mystical gestures such as "foot swivel" and "ski steering," arcane knowledge passed on grudgingly to skiers having "paid their dues" in expensive lift tickets and ski lessons.
turtle	protective position for the body with legs and arms drawn under, assumed after a fall on a crowded slope.

Dreaming about tuning

Unbreakable Crust

U

Ul — Norse god of skiing; can be propitiated only by barbecueing broken ski tips over a fire of P-tex shavings before heading for the slopes. The failure to please Ul can bring on extensive boilerplate and electrical outages.

unbalanced — skier's state of mind when buying ski equipment.

unbreakable crust — April Fool's joke. *That crust is going to break sooner or later, you better believe it!*

uphill — direction in which one vainly tries to turn skis when going too fast.

USSA — *abbr.* United States Ski Association, an invisible organization looking after consumer interests of American skiers.

V

vaunt — word spoken in Austro-American dialect, as *"I vaunt you should keep your skiz togedder!"*

ve — Austrian pronunciation of "we," as *"Now rrright avay, ve schtop dis foolish falling down!"*

velocity	measurement of speed (in miles per hour) on skis: *terminal velocity* is the speed of the skier just before hitting a tree.
vertical drop	total number of feet to the top of a ski resort from the base, measured straight up and rounded off to the next highest 200 feet.
vertigo	dizziness that comes as a natural reaction to being on top of a mountain; may be accompanied by a marked compulsion to lean back. Victims try to develop a keen interest in details of the hat on nearest skier and the snowflakes on the wrist; very dark glasses help.
vest	an armless, insulated parka that can be worn in warmer weather, allows a skier to go days without showering.
veteran	racer over the age of twenty-eight who is convinced that with a little bit of training, he could get right back in there with the kids.
vibration	1. rapid, shaking motion of skis at normal skiing speeds. 2. a rapid, shaking motion of lips at normal skiing temperatures.
video	mobile television camera and projector set, used as a teaching aid so skiers can see themselves ski; comes with handy rack of hara-kiri knives.
view	luxury that one is charged extra for at ski lodges; includes a panorama of rear windows of nearby condos.
Vikings	history's most famous early skiers. They were known to start each other off on a race with a hearty, *"Break a leg, Olaf!"*

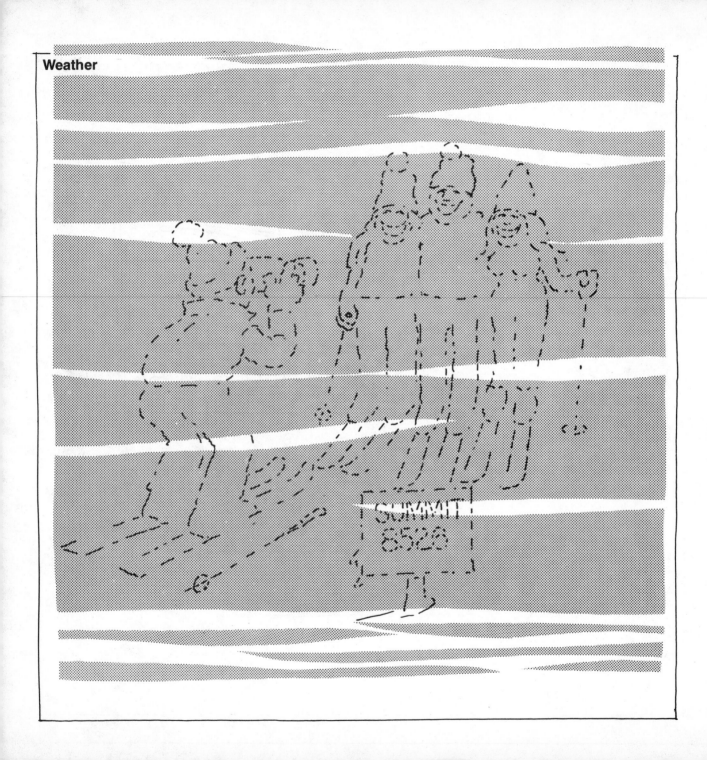

W

wait elapsed time between entering a lift line and getting on the lift. On average, it runs from twenty to forty minutes for a fresh skier, eager to ski down to, oh, four or five minutes for a tired skier in need of rest.

walk technique for beginners on expert terrain.

wallet thick, heavily laden money container that drags the skier down until it is mercifully lightened to an amazing degree at the cafeteria cash register.

warming hut heated shelter on a mountain; a sensible place to spend one's skiing time before the arrival of reasonable temperatures in spring.

warp ski shaping itself in strange twists, giving it an interesting tendency to make turns independent of the actions of owner.

wax substance applied to ski bottoms to cause the weather to change: to create a sudden warming spell, the skier applies a cold-temperature wax; to create a cold spell, he puts on warm-temperature wax; in either case, skis can be walked right down the steepest slopes for a new wax job.

weather factor adding wonderful variety to anyone's skiing experiences. It frequently manifests as a blizzard or downpour to test loyalty to the sport and ability to take abuse.

wedel	sinuous dance performed on skis; native to St. Christoph in the Arlberg; cognoscenti forgo focusing on the sophisticated rolling motion of the hips to study a performer's hands for softness and subtlety of motion.
weight shift	to shift from ski to ski to find one that will turn.
wheelie	freestyle turn in which a skier jerks back to jack the ski tips in air and swivel the skis on their tails; used for last-second avoidance of large objects such as resort restaurants.
whiteout	1. physical disorder causing faulty skiing, brought on by late-night involvement with the likes of "Bloody Mary" and "Tia Maria"; results in an uncontrollable upward rolling of eyeballs to expose the whites of the eyes. 2. a thick, sticky, white gunk used by ski writers to erase results of a congenital incapacity to spell wurds.
windmill	tumbling fall wherein skis flail about like moving blades of a windmill; frequently used by claustrophobic skiers to thin out the crowds in their vicinity.
winter	snow season, traditionally lasting from Thanksgiving to Easter; sometimes postponed to January 15, or ending around February 20; occasionally cancelled altogether. Watch this space for further announcements.
Winter Olympics	quadrennial event that sets new salary levels of amateur skiers from all over world.
World Cup	schedule of races that defines the amateur work year. It extends from the first World Cup races in November until the final races early in April. After that, racers have six months in which to consult stock brokers and financial advisors.

Winter (when skiers bloom)

XC (has a long history)

worm turn

freestyle trick consisting of lying down on the backs of the skis, then rolling over and over while still sliding downhill in a prone position; often involuntarily executed by tourists after a previous night's hearty feasting at a Mexican restaurant.

X

XC

strange cult whose devotees balance on skis narrower than a man's hand in frigid temperatures, courting hypothermia, dehydration, and sore feet.

xenophobia

skier's hatred of strangers, which can strike without warning after 25 minutes in a cafeteria line.

Xmas

holiday featuring incredible lines, crowded slopes, jammed restaurants, and unbelievable lodge prices; appeals to "Xmas nuts" who eagerly book a year ahead at popular resorts.

Xtinct

wool long johns; longthongs; rope tow grippers; heel springs; Northlands; bamboo poles; Head Standards; baggies; $5 lift tickets; Tenth Mountain Division surplus parkas with fur-trimmed hoods; J-bars; single chairs; steel edges fastened with Phillips screws; Tey tape; epoxy bottoms in a bottle. Sigh!

Y

yaw

Nor: yes.

yoicks!	hunting cry of a skier who is rapidly overtaking another and is about to run him to the ground.
yo-yo	1. *v.* to ride repeatedly and rapidly up short lifts and ski down again. 2. *n.* a skier who rides repeatedly and rapidly up short lifts and skis down again.
yump	elevated platform in Norway used to launch skiers into sub-orbital flight.

Z

ze	Austrian pronunciation of English "the," as in "Ben' ze knees, one hundred dollars, pleez."
zigzag	track of an exhausted skier going up or down a slope.
zinc oxide	messy, white coating put on one's nose after trying to create a full winter tan in one day.
zoo	word used to describe busy ski resorts. See *Xmas*.
zoology	scientific study of tourists.
Zzzzz	response during the trip home after a ski weekend, to the following query, "Jack, I seem to have wrenched my back on those last bumps, how about driving for awhile? Jack?"